Baby Bear's Christmas Kiss

To Jack

Other Baby Bear books to share:

Is It Christmas?
Hold Tight!
The Big Baby Bear Book
Number One, Tickle Your Tum

First edition for the United States, its dependencies, the Philippines, and
Canada published in 2004 by Barron's Educational Series, Inc.

First published in Great Britain in 2004 by The Bodley Head,
an imprint of Random House Children's Books

All inquiries should be addressed to:
Barron's Educational Series, Inc.
250 Wireless Boulevard
Hauppauge, New York 11788
http://www.barronseduc.com

International Standard Book No.: 0-7641-5800-7
Library of Congress Catalog Card No.: 2004102087

Printed and bound in Singapore
9 8 7 6 5 4 3 2 1

Baby Bear's Christmas Kiss

JOHN PRATER

It was Christmas Day!
The whole family were visiting Baby Bear and
Grandbear. That's Granny Bear, Uncle Bear,
Auntie Bear, and four Cousin Bears.
The grown-ups warmed up by the fire while the
little ones put their presents under the tree.
But the little ones didn't seem to be
able to leave the presents alone.

Every present was shaken . . .

. . . prodded

. . . and sniffed.

Grandbear had an idea.
"You can open just one
present each, now!"

All the cousins ripped open their presents.

"Wow!" said Baby Bear. "What is it?"
"It's a sled," said Grandbear.
"What's it for?"
asked Baby Bear.
"I'll show you,"
said Uncle Bear.
"Come outside with me."

"Up the hill
we go!"
said Uncle Bear.

"Now watch closely,"
said Uncle Bear.
"First, you . . ."

"Hey!" cried Uncle Bear. "Wait! . . ."

Faster and *faster*
    went Uncle Bear . . .

. . . until he met up with a snowbear!

"That was really funny," said Baby Bear.
"Can we try it now?"

Up the hill
they went again . . .

. . . and down

they came!

Again and again until Uncle Bear said . . .

"Oooh, I can smell yummy cooking.
It's time to go inside."

Grandbear met them at the door.
"Hello, snowbears! You're just
in time for Christmas dinner."

What a feast!

After dinner, the grown-ups were so
full they could hardly move.
The little ones played hide-and-seek.

It didn't take Baby Bear long to find Big Cousin Bear hiding under the tree. "This is my present to Mom and Dad," said Big Cousin Bear. "What are you giving Grandbear?"

"I haven't got a present for Grandbear!" said Baby Bear. "Never mind," said Big Cousin Bear. "It's your turn to hide now!"

While the others covered their eyes and counted to ten, Baby Bear crept out of the room, through the kitchen, and into the garden.

But Baby Bear wasn't hiding. Baby Bear was going to find a present for Grandbear.

Grandbear likes snow, thought Baby Bear.
And stars. Something glistened and caught
Baby Bear's eye . . .

Baby Bear looked closer.
"Snowberries!"
said Baby Bear.
"All twinkly like
the star on the
Christmas
tree!"

Baby Bear picked
some berries, then
started to make
something out
of snow.

When it was
finished,
Baby Bear
hurried
back inside.

"Found you!"
called Cousin Bear.
"Come on, we're opening
the presents now."

Everyone was very excited!

"Merry Christmas,
Grandbear!"
said Baby Bear.
"I brought you
a snowberry
snowbear!"

"Mistletoe!" said
Grandbear. "That
deserves a special
Christmas kiss!
I'll put your lovely
present somewhere
where it won't melt."

All the grown-ups asked

if they could have a

Christmas kiss, too.

The little ones weren't too sure, though.

Merry Christmas, Baby Bear!
Merry Christmas, everyone!

Other Baby Bear books to share:

Is It Christmas?
Hold Tight!
The Big Baby Bear Book
Again!
Walking Round the Garden
Number One, Tickle Your Tum
The Bear Went Over the Mountain
Oh Where, Oh Where?
Clap Your Hands
I'm Coming to Get You!